TWO STARS OF THE SKY

YASHASVI JAISWAL

Contents

Acknowledgements   *v*

1. Chapter 1   1

Acknowledgements

ABOUT THE BOOK

This book is a love story between a surgeon ana a patient . Where surgeon named Ira is a kind of a person who believes in everything is fair in love and war . Hallwach the patient . He was heart patient and he needs a heart transplant but he fails to get .

Ira decided to stole the heart .

Will Ira will be successfull in stealing ?

Will hallwach will survive ?

Let's find out .

ABOUT THE AUTHOR

This book is written by YASHASVI JAISWAL born and brought in Indore , MP . A 17 years old girl believes in , we live only once so do everthing in life atleast once because ' Zindagi badi honi chahiye lambi nhi ' . JAI MATA DI .

1

A Prince charm will come with a beautiful white horse and take away the princess they have their castle and live a perfect live . And the love story ends but this is a lie a big lie ! Hi! My name is Dr. Yashasvi Jaiswal working internship in lifeline hospital with my fellow interns named Olive , Leo , Ira , Henry . This two years of internship period can be the best and worst of your life because 48 hours of shift is not easy at least at first day :) After cardiothoracic surgery , neurosurgery and lot of trauma our first finally ended . In my apartment I was living alone , I need partners so I choose Herny and Ira and I made the mistake a big mistake because they both are like sun and moon they both are completely opposite and opposite attract well !! Only in physics not in real life . They use to fight a lot . The next day , I Herny and Ira assigned to take care of neurosurgery and olive , leo assigned for cardiothoracic surgery. Olive meet the head of cardiothoracic surgery Dr. Lenard . They both have the soft corner for each other . As the time increases there equations is getting better . But one day Dr . Lenard asked olive to move in with him . This was a thunderclap for olive because olive is a messy girl she don't wash her clothes she just buy new one and Dr . Lenard is a neet and clean guy even his herry Potter books are arranged in order . After a lot of trauma they finally moved into one apartment.

They are performing many surgery together and we all are jealous because why not . But its okay at least no one is dying on our watches. One day a patient named Hallwach came in the hospital and Ira takes over the case of Hallwach . His heart was getting week and he wants a heart transplant but his luck was not with him so he went home with some treatment . Time of death 12:43 Being a doctor people live and people die on over watches And you know what I have a obsession With watches in my school timr I borrow watch from my classmates and wear it . Wearing five watches in one hand and six in another. If anyone asks me what's the time ? Being a over dramatic kid I use to say which country time you wants It was very funny but cares I was kid at that time . But not now I have responsibilities of patients..... but no regret because I have power to save lives it's it great . As a newly. Interns we want to be the best and we grew up by listening ' practice makes you best ' . We all want that the patient coming should be under my treatment . With lot of debate the patient in the ambulance will get my treatment means I will get chance to cure him . I was checking his report he was shot by gun , his name was Gargi We decided to remove gun from his chest and Dr. Lenard was operating on him and I got a chance to scrub in . It was a lucky day foe me . I was preparing him for the surgery and I asked hana why your hand inside his chest , she was in ambulance gargi's wife . She said he was bleeding . Then Dr. Lenard notice that the gun that the gun was still inside him and this is not ordinary thing . The gun blast can blast if it will comes in contact with anything and hana's hand was inside him its like cherry on cake . We all got scared and lucky day was not lucky anymore . Being a doctor and I fought for him so I have to be in operation theatre without any disturbance we have to take him to operation theatre which was a big task because the way is not stray but we did it . More difficult task was waiting for us that is to operate him hana started paincing and she wants to leave the room but she was not allowed to do so because if she do then the gun will blast . After trying so hard she quickly removed her hands and she run away but gun didn't blast because my hands were there I couldn't afford this so I got my hands into it . Now the whole hospital is in my hands slowly we did the operation and we took out the gun from his chest . Slowly and steadily win the race . This was the successful operation with lot of complications. But at the end I was proud of myself . Day was ended on good note . The next day Patient was admitted in the hospital his blood pressure was dropping his heart couldn't pump the blood he was having a heart attack . Ira was handling his case . She was reading his reports Patient name Hallwach age 27........ Hallwach was unconscious but Ira was not . Hallwach got by pass surgery . After the surgery he was sleeping and Ira was looking him from side from very long time . She was adoring him . After done with all patients she came to Hallwach as he was awake now . They both saw each other . Ira was a model before her black long hair , her simile was attracting him but they didn't confess each other . Its our lunch time . Lunch time is always fun today we are playing a game in which who eats more chapatti in less time will win the game . In the centre of canteen our gang is eating like animals and peopy are staring us like ghost ..... It was so much fun . We just wait for whole day for lunch so that we can do our nonsense things .... Life is so much better with friends I mean with the real one . After living the 22 years of my life I never got the real one . All of my friends were toxic they were nice on the face and world's worst snake at the back . Especially the school ones . But finally I got the real friends after years . Touchwood..... After doing a lot of fun and weird things its time to get back to the work . We are all got busy with our patients Ira was back in the room of Hallwach What's your name ? .... Hallwach asked Ira Youva ..... She replied Your eyes are so pretty , Hallwach said Ira blushed and went away. All the interns were in the changing room , changing there scrub . Ira enter we started teasing Ira but she was not ready to accept it we all were laughing .... Then chief enters He was 6 feet tall and he looks so dangerous . He shouted on all of us ' what's happening here is joke to you . You are responsible doctors you are not allowed to do so , You have lives to save , lives to treat' , we all were seeing each other faces , truly said internship years can be the best and the worst and we saw both the sides . We went back on our floors... Leo got his posting in gynaecology department which he hates the most . Lady giving birth, that scream , that pain he hates a lot . But he has to do because it his job .... After the intense work the day was over and we went back to home . We were so tired but happy as well ! So no regrets. The next day Ira was asked to take CT of Hallwach she was taking him . They were in lift . You didn't answered me in funny way Hallwach said Silence is the best answer said Ira and laughed. His CT was done the result were out . Result was , shocking his heart is becoming so week day by day he needs a good heart he needs a heart transplant. But there is no one who could donate him . Dr. Lenard decide to give him more attention and said Ira to take care more of Hallwach . He was listed in the donation list . But on the 2nd number . We live once , we die once and we love once . Ira was in loving phase . I am felling very bad for Ira . She was loving man who has very less amount of time. But there love is unconditional . Love has no limits . But I am happy for Ira also because nowadays there is hard to find . And for me I think its impossible because I always choose wrong man and ended up having a toxic relationship . But its okay we learn from our mistake and now I am happily single . Ira was giving her most of the time to Hallwach . She was giving her best to get him well but all her affords were wasting because there is no improvement in his health . By the time a good news came . A heart is donated by someone and Hallwach can take it . The donor was died in the accident . Dr. Lenard and olive went in the Harvard hospital for that where lenard's very old friend works . Olive was getting jealous for that . Ira was just praying for him but sadly it didn't worked because when lenard was taking it out he notice that he has hole in his heart Wall and it is of no use now . Hallwach couldn't take it With a heavy heart Dr. Lenard and olive was back in hospital . There faces were pale , disappointment was reflecting on tere faces . Ira was just crying to the hell . It was very hard for Ira to believe in it . It was Ira's last hope . She has done many nice things in her past but in return she was not getting it . She use to believe in karma but not anymore . Who do good and gets good in return its not necessary . All four of us were trying to cherr up Ira but it was not working a bit . All these things was noticed by the chief who seem death to us and there is a rule in hospital that doctor and patient can't cross there line and Ira did it earlier. She made the bond which was hard to separate . Ira wad told not to handle this case any more that case was given to Henry but why she will listen to chief because she becomed Juliet Hallwach was the Romeo . She fights and take over that Case again . She snatched . Christmas was near Ira loves Christmas we made cookies , decorated house , made Christmas trees , buyed her dress for her . Herny and I surprised her . After twelve days we saw a lil smile on Ira's face . This thing was done by me , it's a big deals because I didn't like Christmas . But I was happy to see her happy . We celebrate Christmas we were dancing , having dinner , we saw Ira happy after a lot of time I was happy after seeing her . And we slept under the Christmas tree . This morrow is a thunderclap for Ira. She got up in morning , she went to take shower , made breakfast , today she was a bit late . She was not feeling well today . With a heavy heart she took her step towards the hospital . Today the luck of Ira was not with her first her breakfast was lack of Salt so it was tasteless and then her car was not working . After many attempt it managed to start . Then she meet the traffic . She was pissed off . But finally after many struggle she reached hospital . The scene she saw there was terrible its like ground was on head . She couldn't digest it . There was a code blue . The cry of Ira was so loud that every member of hospital can listen it . Ira was fainting again and again . Hallwach had his 2 nd silent heart attack . And you know what silent attack is worst because in that you can'tsre any symptoms . It is very painful . I can feel Ira . Because my grandma was also a heart patient , she also had attack and she left us forever . We couldn't save her . She was very close me and I still wear those gloves that she made for me . No matter that the gloves are small now . Hallwach was taken into operation room . Doctors were tensed they were not able to think to what to do . On the other hand Ira was getting glucose bottles . Doctor first decide to go for by pass but it will not worth it , his heart couldn't afford it . Life is hard after seeing Hallwach and Ira I think my life is sort of nice . Finally after a long struggle doctor decide to put him on LVAD (Left ventricular assist device) . It can give him life for two or more than that . For this operation someone have to sign some forms but Hallwach father lives in USA and his mother is passed away four years ago due to cancer there is no family member to sign the forms . After Ira got the this information she immediately signed it . So clearly Ira is his family now . Ira is a surgeon she knows advantages and disadvantages of LVAD she was afraid but she was happy also that atleast it will give him life they will get more time to spend . Anaesthesiologist gave him anaesthesia , batteries successfully installed in his body operation went successful . But still he in in ICU (intensive care unit) he is under observation od Dr. Lenard . Dr. Lenard is a successful cardiologist in the town . He done many surgery nicely . He is one the best surgeon . Ira has a faith in him , she knows that Hallwach is in good hands . In ICU there is a rule that anybody can not enter in room with this Ira is not allowed to enter so she use to watch him from the glass window and passes him smile . After 2-3 days he was shifted back in the private ward . Ira was the happiest person in the town . Dr. Lenard was giving him instructions to not to run , he can't stand for long hours , he can't walk for few days . You have to take care of his diet lenard told ira . He can't have fatty things give him fruit and healthy food . Make sure he do not have alcohol , cigarette and other stuff . You are responsible for his diet said Dr. Lenard . Ok sir ...... Ira Will see you soon.......Dr. Lenard Congratulations! You survived.... Ira said with laughter. But your looks can kill me ....Hallwach Ira smiled.... They were talking and I was seeing them form outside and I am thinking why I don't have someone like him . But no regret because when I had someone he cheated on me badly and now I don't like love and relationship . At this moment I was happy for Ira . I never saw her this happy . There vibes are matching to next level . Ira was spending her most of the time with him .

Being a surgeon she had to perform surgeries as well as to take care to him . She do her rounds in morning and spend time with him in evening . She do lunch with him , dinner with him . Hallwach was looking happy for outside only not from the inside . He is stressed out from inside but he was not showing it out especially in front of front of Ira. He wants her to be happy and not to be tensed because to him . They spent time together since morning now Ira have to leave . She was not ready to go but rules can't be changed . Next morning , She was so excited to meet Hallwach that she woke up up two hours before her usual time . She loves to cooks so she made breakfast for him . She went for the hospital early today . As soon as she run towards Hallwach . Every member of the hospital is looking at her like she run from mental hospital or she has some kind of mental disorder . They both were extremely happy to see each other . Good morrow.... Ira This is too early......Hallwach You have to live a healthy lifestyle..... Ira said and laughed . Okay! So have breakfast and take care I am going on rounds see you soon ..... Ira I will be waiting..... Hallwach Chief niece was admitted in hospital that day she was very young suffering from cancer . She has very less time . She has a dream of having a huge dreamy prom . So chief decided of having it . Preparation of doing it was given to Leo and henry . 11:30 lunch time As Hallwach and Ira loves to spend time with each other . They both loves to play games together, having cupcakes . So what's your likes and dislikes .... Hallwach Ummmm I like doing calligraphy, cooking but only Indian food , I love to interact with new people there culture and I don't like people who hide things from me and compare me with others because I believe in garden every flower is unique and beautiful you can't say lily or rose is the best . What about you......Ira I am very simple guy who loves the lady sitting in front in me. Ira blushed Your pick up lines are so good . Any past relationship ? .... Hallwach Yaa... it's better not to talk about it . I had my worst experience . Don't be sad . Ira was paged by chief and she left the room . It was emergency Hysterectomy (removal of uterus) . Ira was surbing in they performed surgery and went so well . It was a lunch time we all interns were discussing about the day . Me and leo got the duty of decoration for the prom of chief's niece .... Herny . Please don't mess that like your life ..... olive Just stup up ...... Herny This is gonna be better than your face .... Herny . Stop fighting like baby ..... leo What shall we choose the colour and theme ? .... Leo Herny : white? Olive : You are such a boring person ! Go for black and golden . Herny : No Olive : End of discussion . Leo : okay! We are going with black and golden . The next morning , Hallwach was very tired of being in just one room . He had a life but he is not living it to the fullest . He decided to go for a walk . Doctors strictly said he can't climb the stairs . But he did . He went on the stairs and he fell down . He fainted . He was trying to escape the problems . Team came and took him in the room and stabilized him . Why you have done this ? You know you can't climb the stairs and after even knowing that you did he . Why ? Tell me ..... Ira Ira anger was on the 7 th level . I am not happy with my life at all . Its like I have a body but not soul , my soul is missing Ira I want to explore the world . But how with having two batteries on my back ? I can't walk , I can't run. I am living the worst and boring phase of my life . I need a heart, a good heart , a heart with I can explore the world , see the world. I don't want this batteries . This was the emotional breakdown of Hallwach . I promise I will do my best to get you that ...... Ira . Lenard : I have good news for you Ira . Ira: What ? Lenard : We got the heart . Ira : What ! Finally!!!!! My happiness is on 9th cloud right now . Lenard : We are going tomorrow . As a surgeon People think our lives is so easy so amazing people come , bless and go but this is not true . You have someone's life in your hand . Dealing with that pressure we work , we serve . Having someone's life who is very close to you is worst . No one believe that there life will turn out just kind of okay . We all think we're going to be great and from the day we decide to be surgeon we filled with expectations. Exceptions of the trails will blaze . The people we will help , the difference will make , great expectations of who we will be where we will go . The next day , The day started very well . Lenard went for heart with leo . Ira was left behind in the hospital she was not happy with this but she was emotionally attached to Hallwach . Lenard reached the hospital and there whole sence was different . There was one more patient who was waiting for the heart . In the list od people who needs organ Hallwach was on the 2nd place with just 17 seconds . Means Hallwach was just 17 seconds late . Lenard knows the condition of Hallwach and he don't want to let go this heart . He was trying his best to take it . There Ira wad tense , she was trying to connect with leo and lenard but they both are busy that he can't pick her calls . Both the patient were under observation and they both badly needs heart . As soon as Ira's call got connected to leo , he told everything to Ira . Ira started panicking , she started telling lie fo leo . But they both were friends since a very long time so he knows that Ira is lying . Leo : Are you trying to fool me Ira : Give phone to lenard Leo : Don't you dare to do wrong thing Ira : Just give phone to lenard Ira was a girl who believes in everything is fair in love and war . She told lenard that Hallwach blood pressure is dropping , his lungs is crashing , his organ were slowing down the process . She lied to lenard . After she told this authority have to give him heart to lenard but they need proof which Ira don't have . Being a believer in everything is fair in love and war . Ira decide to cut the wire of LVAD . She told all the procedure to Hallwach and explained him . Ira's plan was to cut the wire of LVAD and the condition of Hallwach will go down . Hospital have to give him heart . Ira was scared . Hallwach told Ira …. I am already living my life worst I don't care if I die . Atleast I have someone who loves me . Don't be afraid you are not going to die . Just believe in me , have faith in me . I believe in you that's why I have given thread of my life to you . We are together and will be together ….. Ira . Ira's hand were shivering Don't be afraid come on let's do this , come on Ira you are brave . Ira cutted the wire of LVAD ……….. She informed Dr. Lenard that Hallwach condition is going down . She lied to him . Basically she stolen a heart . Dr lenard was returning back but it was very difficult because there was huge fight and stampede was going on , guns were shooting , people were going mad . Love is blind people don't see what wrong and right in love . People who is in love for them everything is correct , everything they are doing is right . Ira was thinking she is doing right but off course not . She done a crime . And obviously she can't tell this to hospital so she decided to take the help of us . Ira called all of us in room . As we are interns we still have a lot to learn . As olive was working under Dr . Lenard 24x7 she knows more than all of us . Ira pleased olive that please help me to get back him . This is against rule . Olive was not ready to take any action . Then we all told olive . After a long debate olive finally ready to do the help . We all were helping her someone is giving him shock , someone is giving him CPR But wrong thing can't be hidden for a long time it comes out . Chief was already getting hint that something wrong is happening he could sense it but now he is front of us .

We all are looking at him and he was looking at us . He was so angry that he turned red . What is happening here chief asked . Silence...... Move Hallwach to operation room and call Lenard immediately .... Chief . Herny called lenard Where are you sir ? On the way here is so much rush get the operation room ready I am coming . Lenard was rushing to the hospital but destiny has some other plan . Lenard was shoot on his right shoulder . He was the only surgeon who has perfect in heart transplant . He is the only hope that Ira had . As somebody said if bad things happen good thing will also happens . Lenard was shoot that have seen by some of hospital member. They immediately taken him to hospital. Dr. Lenard was taken to the operation room. His operation was going on, on the other hand other surgeon was called for his surgery. He already had so much of stress and his age was making the surgery complicated, surgeons were in the problem because he is loosing blood and he has AB type of blood group which is rare blood group in the world. Doctors were trying their best to gave him life, they cutted him, operated, removed his old heard and putted a new one but it is not easy as saying there were so many complications. Doctor putted the heart but it was not pumping the blood. Charge 200... All clear Charged 200 Shock The straight line went up and down, he is back in game. His surgery went good, Dr. Lenard surgery was also successful as hallwach was taking rest there were no one allowed to meet. After 24 hours, Dr. Lenard and Hallwach woke up. Ira was so excited to meet him. So she made lunch for him and went. So have lunch... Ira Good to see you without battery... Ira Me too, world is nice without battery.. Hallwach You have done crime, I hope it doesn't effect your career... Hallwach Who cares... Ira At this moment I just want you in my life, I have talent I will earn it, I don't care about money, I will earn it again, But I can't earn you back. Honestly, you can't have someone more than money and career. So let's forget this I have good news to tell you... Ira. What?... I can't wait just tell me quickly Tomorrow we have prom in hospital : Ira Hallwach : In hospital! Ira: yaa.. chief niece is suffering from cancer and she had very less time and she had dream very less time and she had dream of having Prom. Hallwach : ohhh... So should I wear pink or black, Ira just wear white gown Hallwach. I have something to talk about... Hallwach Ira: just tell Hallwach : I know you're the only one I want to share the rest of my life with, The story of our love is only beginning, let's write our own happy ending, there are many ways to be happy in this but all I really need is you . So miss Ira will you marry me? You will be Mrs Ira Hallwach? Waiting for your answer. Ira : Every girl has a dream of kind of proposal. You are so cheesy I loved this . Hallwach : Answer Ira : off course yes. So tomorrow chief's niece will have her prom and will exchange our rings... Hallwach Yes... Ira The next day, Ira was excited... She wrote a white chown with red rose on her hair and she decided to surprise Hallwach. Whole hospital was busy in prom. They were dancing, singing, playing games. Ira took a ring which says forever. On the other side Hallwach was taking his last breathes, in his last time he wrote a note. Dear Ira , The day I saw you I fall for you, I don't know that we will see each other again or not but memories are with me forever, my gut feeling is saying, I am guest of just few hours, I was excited to see you in that white dress, I was excited to dance on our favourite song 'perfect'. I know it your dream to dance on that song on your big day but I am sorry... You are only one who helped me in my bad time, so you deserve my love, care, respect and this is all you are my dearest, so I am giving all my money and property to you, from now the money and property is all yours, The cheque of 1.8 million USD is kept under the pillow with the ring that I brought for you. With love Yours Hallwach While writing this hallwach took his last breath. Ira was eagerly waiting for the reaction of Hallwach in that white dress. Ira left home and she was coming into the hospital, Hallwach in that white dress, After writing the letter, Hallwach slept and never wake up. Ira reached the hospital, everybody was giving her compliment but she was waiting for the only one compliment, that she wants to hear from Hallwach. She reached to room of Hallwach. The scene was painful. Nurses were removing all the syringe from his body. Time of death, 8:02. Ira was ready to believe this, she was not getting a second that tears are not coming out from her eyes, the condition Ira was terrible. Death is a bitter truth that everyone has to accept and is hard to believe and for Ira it was hardest to believe that the day she became bride the same day she will be widow How hard it was for her to digest this. She almost scarfed everything, her career for a person who is no more. Ira couldn't control herself , Hallwach was everything for her. The work she did was incredible, she saved so many lives, with that note hospital called her back. After 17 days, Ira back a surgeon , she was back in game, it was hard phase for her . She donated that 1.8 million to the hospital for the needy people and people who couldn't afford the surgery she do for free of cost. Two shiny beautiful stars of the sky became one. Hallwach left the world and Ira lived in his memories, she proudly lived as widow of Mr Hallwach.